WITHDRAWN

Anne Arundel Co. Public Library

W9-BRB-463

TO NAKOA

FERN
and
HORN

MARIE-LOUISE GAY

GROUNDWOOD BOOKS
HOUSE OF ANANSI PRESS
TORONTO   BERKELEY

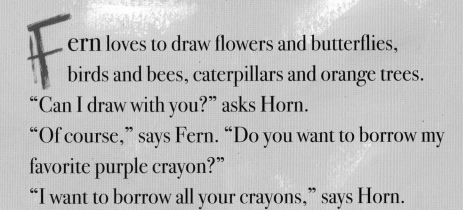

Fern loves to draw flowers and butterflies,
birds and bees, caterpillars and orange trees.
"Can I draw with you?" asks Horn.
"Of course," says Fern. "Do you want to borrow my
favorite purple crayon?"
"I want to borrow all your crayons," says Horn.

But Horn thinks that his flowers look like purple pancakes.
That his caterpillars look like striped socks.
That his birds look like witches' hats.

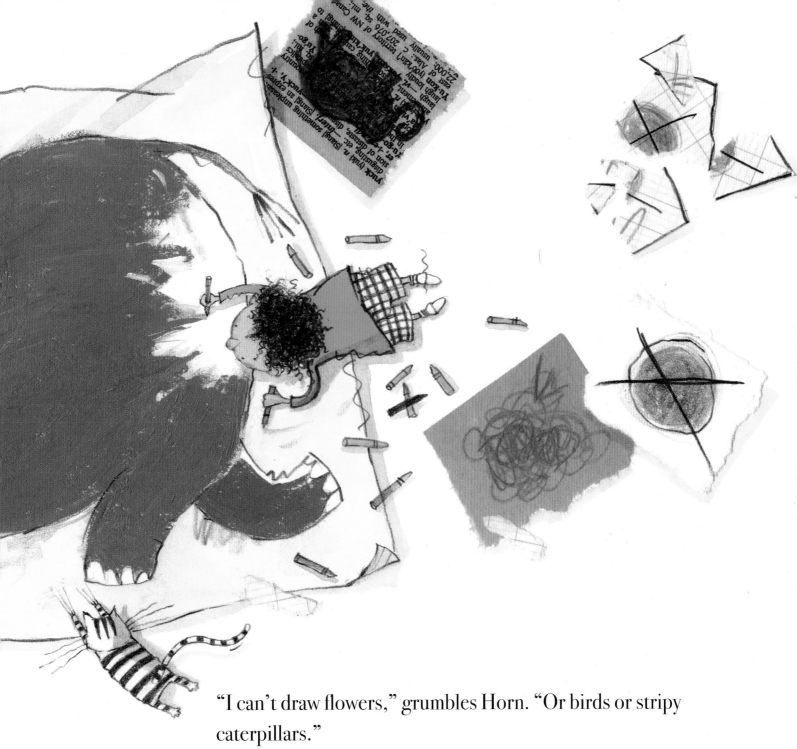

"I can't draw flowers," grumbles Horn. "Or birds or stripy caterpillars."

"Draw whatever you want," says Fern.

"Elephants!" says Horn. "I'm good at drawing elephants."

The problem
is that Horn's
elephant is big
and ferocious.
It loves to stomp
on Fern's flowers and swallow
her butterflies, birds and bees,
caterpillars and orange trees.

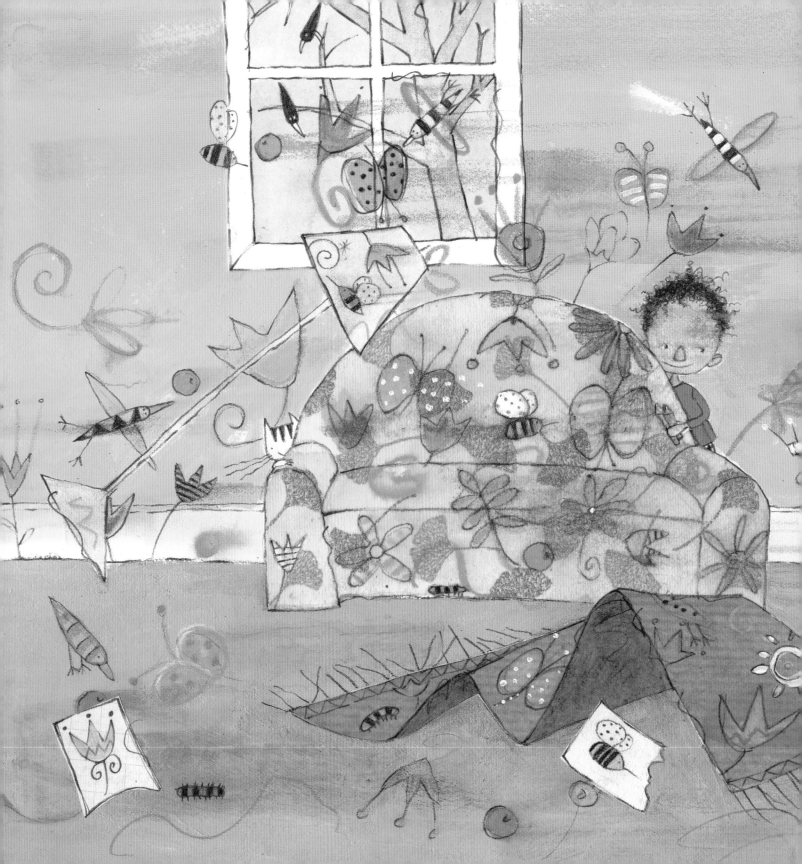

"Uh-oh," says Horn. "What happened here?"
"You know what happened here," sighs Fern.
"You should keep your elephant on a leash."

Luckily, Fern's imagination is as big as the earth.
As big as the sky.
As big as the universe.

Fern loves looking at stars. They sparkle and glow from a
million light years away. Sometimes she hears them singing.
Fern also loves making stars.

She cuts out bright morning stars, fiery shooting stars
and even starfish. She sprinkles stardust everywhere.
Fern hangs the stars so high that not even
a ferocious elephant could reach them.
"Can I make some stars too?" asks Horn.
"Of course," says Fern. "Do you want to borrow my
scissors?"
"Yes," answers Horn.

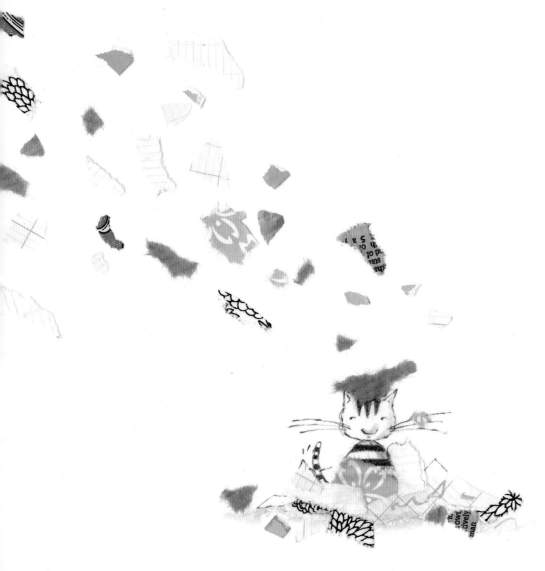

But Horn thinks his stars look like confetti. Or giant snowstorms or macaroni (without cheese, of course). "I can't make stars," grumbles Horn. "Your scissors are way too slippery."

"Do you want me to help you?" asks Fern.

"No," says Horn. He has another idea.

He tears and rips. He glues and snips.

Horn makes an enormous wild polar bear.

The polar bear gobbles up the bright morning stars.

It devours the fiery shooting stars and the starfish.

It licks up every little speck of stardust with its bright pink tongue.

"Uh-oh!" says Horn. "What happened here?"
"You know very well what happened here," sighs Fern.
"You need to teach your polar bear some good manners."

Luckily, Fern's
imagination is as big
as the earth.
As big as the sky.
As big as the universe.

She thinks and thinks. She sketches and draws.
"I know!" says Fern. "I will build the biggest, strongest castle
in the world. A castle that will stand up against polar bear
gobbles and elephant stomps."

"Horn! Do you want to help me?" Fern calls out.
But Horn doesn't answer. He has disappeared into thin air.
He has another, better idea.

Fern builds a magnificent castle with turrets and a dark dungeon. In front there is a deep moat where a hungry shark swims in circles.

Meanwhile, Horn pulls out a long, green, scaly thing from the bottom drawer of his dresser. He puts it on and sneaks out into the yard.

At almost the exact same moment, a great bat-winged,
fire-breathing dragon attacks the castle.

Fern is ready. She knows what dragons like to eat.
Chocolate chip cookies!
She throws a handful of cookies at the dragon.

The dragon is delighted.
He is so busy devouring the cookies that he steps
into the moat.
The shark bites the dragon's big toe.

"Uh-oh," says Fern. "What happened here?"
"Ouch! Ouch! Ouch!" says Horn. "Your shark bit my big toe!"
"Do you want another cookie?" asks Fern.

"I'm going to build a rocket ship next," says Fern.
"The fastest rocket ship in the universe."
"I'm going to make a monster from outer space,"
says Horn. "With three eyes and four arms."

Copyright © 2019 by Marie-Louise Gay
Published in Canada and the USA in 2019 by Groundwood Books

All rights reserved. No part of this publication may be reproduced, stored in a
retrieval system or transmitted, in any form or by any means, without the prior
written consent of the publisher or a license from The Canadian Copyright
Licensing Agency (Access Copyright). For an Access Copyright License, visit
www.accesscopyright.ca or call toll free to 1-800-893-5777.

Groundwood Books / House of Anansi Press
groundwoodbooks.com

We gratefully acknowledge for their financial support of our publishing
program the Canada Council for the Arts, the Ontario Arts Council and the
Government of Canada.

Canada Council   Conseil des Arts
for the Arts   du Canada

ONTARIO ARTS COUNCIL
CONSEIL DES ARTS DE L'ONTARIO
an Ontario government agency
un organisme du gouvernement de l'Ontario

With the participation of the Government of Canada
Avec la participation du gouvernement du Canada   Canadä

Library and Archives Canada Cataloguing in Publication
Gay, Marie-Louise, author, illustrator
Fern and Horn / Marie-Louise Gay.
ISBN 978-1-77306-226-6 (hardcover)
I. Title
PS8563.A868F47 2019   jC813'.54   C2018-906576-1

The illustrations were done in acrylic, watercolor, HB and 6B pencil and collage.
Design by Michael Solomon
Printed and bound in Malaysia

FSC
www.fsc.org
MIX
Paper from
responsible sources
FSC® C012700